THIS CANDLEWICK BOOK BELONGS TO:

_____

_____

_____

_____

For Susan, Limulus rescuer and eloquent e-mailer
R. H.

For my grandmothers, Margaret and Rose
K. K.

Text copyright © 2000 by Ruth Horowitz
Illustrations copyright © 2000 by Kate Kiesler

First paperback edition 2004

The Library of Congress has cataloged the hardcover edition as follows:

Horowitz, Ruth.
Crab moon / Ruth Horowitz ; illustrated by Kate Kiesler.
p.   cm.
Summary: One June night, a young boy watches as many, many horseshoe crabs
come ashore to lay their eggs.
ISBN 978-0-7636-0709-8 (hardcover)
1. Limulus polyphemus — Juvenile fiction. [1. Horseshoe crabs — Fiction.]
I. Kiesler, Kate, ill. II. Title.
PZ10.3H787 Cr 2000
[E] — dc21   99-047077

ISBN 978-0-7636-2313-5 (paperback)

12 13 14 15 SCP 12 11 10 9

Printed in Humen, Dongguan, China

This book was typeset in Opti Cather.
The illustrations were done in oils.

Candlewick Press
99 Dover Street
Somerville, Massachusetts 02144

visit us at www.candlewick.com

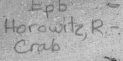

crab moon

Ruth Horowitz

illustrated by Kate Kiesler

CANDLEWICK PRESS

The summer Daniel turned seven, his family rented a cottage at the beach. They arrived on the weekend of the full moon.

"The full moon in June brings the high tide of the horseshoe crabs," said his mother. "I saw them laying their eggs on this beach when I was your age."

"Does it still happen?" Daniel asked.

"Every summer," his mother answered. "Horseshoe crabs have been coming ashore for hundreds of millions of years. They're older than the dinosaurs."

"Can I see them?" Daniel asked.

"You'll have to get up in the middle of the night. I'll come and wake you," she promised.

That night, the fat, round face
of the full moon wavered
on the surface of the water.
The path felt cool under
Daniel's feet. As the beam of
their flashlight swept the
beach, he drew a sharp breath.

Everywhere they looked, horseshoe crabs crowded and pushed, like restless cobblestones. Under the sandy shuffle of the surf, he could hear the clack of the crabs' shielded backs bumping and scraping together.

Near Daniel's feet, a large crab dug in the sand.

"That's a female," his mother said. "The smaller crab on her back is a male. She laid her eggs in that hole, and now she's pulling him across so he can fertilize them." They watched as the female crab swung herself around. Still carrying her mate, she made her way back to the water.

Little by little, the tide receded. The crabs returned
to the sea. Daniel's feet sank into the sand as he and
his mother climbed back up to bed.

In the morning, Daniel raced
back to the beach. The tide
was low, now. The crabs were
gone. Curly black seaweed
was strewn on the sand, like
streamers left over from a party.

Then Daniel saw one last, lonely crab marooned upside down. She looked dead and dry. He found a piece of driftwood and gently nudged her. One leg moved. The other crabs had scratched their tracks in the sand where they had swung themselves around and gone home.

How could this crab follow unless someone turned her over?

Daniel reached out one nervous
finger. The tail felt stiff, but
not sharp. He carefully lifted
the crab.

As her body left the ground,
her claws started to snap.
Daniel put her down fast.

Then he took a deep breath
and reached for her again.
This time, he quickly turned
the crab over, and gently
set her down.

Daniel grinned.

Barnacles and slipper shells covered the crab's back, like jewels on a crown. She set off down the beach, pausing, and pulling her shell through the sand, quiet as a queen.

Slowly and grandly, the crab pulled herself forward. Stepping and pausing, Daniel's feet felt their way into the bay. He followed until she disappeared. Then he gave the water one last, long look and whispered to his horseshoe crab, "See you next summer."

About Horseshoe Crabs

◆ Horseshoe crabs have lived, virtually unchanged, for more than 350 million years. They are not really crabs at all. Their scientific name is *Limulus polyphemus*, and their closest living relatives are scorpions, spiders, and other joint-legged animals called arthropods.

◆ Horseshoe crabs' hard shells protect their soft undersides from predators. Their long, pointed tails help them steer as they move over sand and through water. Their six pairs of claws are useful for grabbing the sea worms and mollusks they eat.

◆ Each spring, horseshoe crabs begin their long journey over miles of ocean floor toward the sheltered beaches where they spawn. They may be found from Maine to Mexico. The largest horseshoe crab crowds gather at Delaware Bay.

◆ A single female crab may lay up to 70,000 eggs in her lifetime. The huge number of eggs not only ensures another generation of horseshoe crabs, but also the survival of certain species of shore birds. Each year, thousands of these birds fly 6,000 miles from the tip of South America to their nesting grounds in the Arctic tundra. They reach Delaware Bay, the halfway point of their migration, just as the crabs arrive. The crabs' fat-rich eggs provide a feast for the birds—and the energy they need to complete their journey.

◆ People also depend on horseshoe crabs. Scientists use horseshoe crabs' unique blood to test medicines and diagnose certain diseases. Ninety percent of crabs used for medical purposes are returned to the sea to produce another generation of horseshoe crabs.

◆ Unfortunately, horseshoe crab populations are plummeting as their spawning grounds are destroyed and as they are killed for use as bait. Not surprisingly, the numbers of shore birds who depend on horseshoe crab eggs have also declined dramatically.

RUTH HOROWITZ grew up in New Jersey, spent part of her childhood in France, and now lives in Vermont. *Crab Moon* is her third book for children. "I'm drawn to species that get overlooked because they're not big-eyed or cuddly or cute. I hope this book will show readers the rewards of reaching out to a being that may seem utterly alien at first glance."

KATE KIESLER studied illustration at the Rhode Island School of Design. She makes her home in the mountains of Colorado, but enjoyed painting the seashore for this book. "On a snowy day I could walk into my studio and be at the beach. Sometimes I could almost smell the salty air."